D1309033

For Alexandra and Francesca Harrod—J. K.
For Mark—J. R.

ERC
Juv.
PZ
7
.K1297
Do
1993

Text copyright © 1993 by Jacqueline Karas
Illustrations copyright © 1993 by Judith Riches
First published in Great Britain by ABC, All Books for
Children, a division of The All Children's Company Ltd.

All rights reserved. No part of this book may be reproduced
or utilized in any form or by any means, electronic or
mechanical, including photocopying, recording, or by any
information storage or retrieval system, without permission in
writing from the Publisher.
Inquiries should be addressed to
Tambourine Books, a division of William Morrow & Company, Inc.,
1350 Avenue of the Americas, New York, New York 10019.
Printed and bound in Hong Kong

Library of Congress Cataloging in Publication Data

Karas, Jacqueline. The doll house / by Jacqueline Karas;
illustrated by Judith Riches.—1st U.S. ed. p. cm.
Summary: Alexandra gradually befriends the Toy family that has
moved into her doll house, but when her rough cousin breaks their
things, the family decides to move.
[1. Dolls—Fiction.] I. Riches, Judith, ill. II. Title.
PZ7.K1297Do1993 [E]—dc20 92-32262 CIP AC
ISBN 0-688-12480-1.—ISBN 0-688-12481-X (lib. bdg.)
1 3 5 7 9 10 8 6 4 2
FIRST U.S. EDITION

20766589

MANKATO STATE UNIVERSITY
MEMORIAL LIBRARY
MANKATO, MINNESOTA

The Doll House

Jacqueline Karas · pictures by Judith Riches

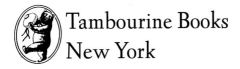
Tambourine Books
New York

RECEIVED

MAR 1 4 1995

MSU - LIBRARY

One morning, Alex opened her eyes and saw a tiny moving van pull up outside her doll house.

Out stepped a little bear wearing a hat with daisies and carrying a suitcase.

The bear walked up to the front door, opened it, and stepped inside. Two small dolls and a red velvet pony pushing a trunk went in next.

Alex got out of bed and looked through one of the doll house windows.

A small, angry face appeared and the curtains closed.

"School!" said Alex's mother, coming into her room.

Alex watched the house until it was time to leave, but nothing else happened.

As soon as she got home, Alex ran upstairs to her room. Now there was a white picket fence all around the doll house. A sign had been nailed to the gate. It said NO TRESPASSERS ALLOWED.

Alex heard noises coming from inside. She watched the house until bedtime, but didn't see a thing.

When she got home from school the next day, Alex saw that a tree had been planted in the front garden and a flower border circled the lawn.

Each day there was something new.

Sometimes, when she went to bed, Alex saw bright lights in the house and heard a radio playing music.

Sometimes the windows and the gate were open.

Once there was a tiny bicycle under the kitchen window and a jump rope hanging over the fence.

One day Alex found a small blue shoe under her bed. She put it on the front step of the doll house and knocked gently with one finger on the front door.

A little hand appeared and whisked the shoe inside.

The next morning Alex found a stamp-sized envelope on her pillow. The card inside said "Thank you" and was signed "The Toy Family."

From then on Alex got along fine with her new neighbors. She never peeked through the windows, and they stopped closing the curtains.

She didn't let her puppy play
in the room because he frightened
the velvet pony, and the Toys
stopped shutting their front door.

When Alex's mother put up
new wallpaper in the living room,
Alex placed unused pieces outside
the Toys' back door. Later, she
could see a very sticky bear and
pony decorating their hallway.

Everything was fine until Alex's cousin Martin came to visit. Martin was *awful*. He played with Alex's doll house and, because he was a guest, Alex couldn't stop him.

He pulled up the tiny flower beds and parked his collection of toy cars on the carpet lawn.

He threw the Toys' furniture into the bathtub and broke their beds.

He even took the velvet pony outside and left him there. It took the pony two days to find his way home.

Alex couldn't wait for Martin to go home. She rushed upstairs to tell the Toy family as soon as he left.

But the curtains were closed, the front door was shut, and there was a FOR SALE sign nailed to the front gate.

The Toys were gone and not even their good-bye present of a tiny picture book, wrapped in gold paper and left on her pillow, could cheer up Alex.

Every night, she watched the doll house for lights and listened for music.

Every morning when she woke up, she hoped to see a bicycle or a shoe.

Every afternoon after school, she looked to see if the curtains were open again.

SOLD

Finally, one day there was something different.
There was a new sign on the gate. It said SOLD.